THE AMAZING BONE

THE AMAZING BONE

· WILLIAM STEIG ·

A SUNBURST BOOK · FARRAR, STRAUS AND GIROUX

To Maggie, Melinda, Francesca, and Nika

It was a brilliant day, and instead of going straight home from school, Pearl dawdled. She watched the grownups in town at their grownup work, things she might someday be doing.

She saw the street cleaners sweeping the streets and she looked in at the bakery on Parsnip Lane and saw the bakers taking hot loaves of pumpernickel out of the oven and powdering crullers with sugar dust.

On Cobble Road she stopped at Maltby's barn and stood gawking as the old gaffers pitched their ringing horseshoes and spat tobacco juice.

Later she sat on the ground in the forest between school and home, and spring was so bright and beautiful, the warm air touched her so tenderly, she could almost feel herself changing into a flower. Her light dress felt like petals.

"I love everything," she heard herself say.

"So do I," a voice answered.

Pearl straightened up and looked around. No one was there. "Where are you?" she asked.

"Look down," came the answer. Pearl looked down. "I'm the bone in the violets near the tree by the rock on your right."

Pearl stared at a small bone. "You talk?" she murmured.

"In any language," said the bone. "¿Habla español? Rezumiesh popol-

sku? Sprechen sie Deutsch? And I can imitate any sound there is." The bone made the sounds of a trumpet calling soldiers to arms. Then it sounded like wind blowing, then like pattering rain. Then it snored, then sneezed.

Pearl couldn't believe what she was hearing. "You're a bone," she said. "How come you can sneeze?"

"I don't know," the bone replied. "I didn't make the world."

"May I take you home with me, wonderful bone?" Pearl asked.

"You certainly may," said the bone. "I've been alone a long time. A year ago, come August, I fell out of a witch's basket. I could have yelled after her as she walked on, but I didn't want to be her bone any longer. She ate snails cooked in garlic at every meal and was always complaining about her rheumatism and asking nosy questions. I'd be happier with someone young and lively like you."

Pearl picked the bone up and gently put it in her purse. She left the purse open, so they could continue their talk, and started home, forgetting her schoolbooks on the grass. She was eager to show this bone to

her parents, and she could guess what would happen when she did. She would tell about the talking bone, her mother would say "You're only imagining it," her father would agree, and then the bone would flabbergast them both by talking.

The spring green sparkled in the spring light. Tree toads were trilling. "It's the kind of wonderful day," said Pearl, "when wonderful things happen—like my finding you."

"Like *my* finding *you*!" the bone answered. And it began to whistle a walking tune that made the going very pleasant.

But not for long. Who should rush out from in back of a boulder and spoil everything but three highway robbers with pistols and daggers. Pearl couldn't tell what breed of animal they were, because they wore cloaks and Halloween masks, but they were fierce and spoke in chilling voices.

"Hand over the purse!" one commanded. Pearl would have gladly surrendered the purse, just to be rid of them, but not with the bone in it.

"You can't have my purse," she said, surprised at her own boldness.
"What's in it?" said another robber, pointing his gun at Pearl's head.

"I'm in it!" the bone growled. And it began to hiss like a snake and roar like a lion.

The robbers didn't wait around to hear the rest, in case there was any more. They fled so fast you couldn't tell which way they'd gone. It made Pearl laugh. The bone, too.

They continued on their way, joking about what had just happened and chatting about this and that. But it wasn't long before a fox stepped forth from behind a tree and barred their path. He wore a sprig of lilac in his lapel, he carried a cane, and he was grinning so the whole world could see his sharp white teeth.

"Hold everything," he said. Pearl froze. "You're exactly what I've been longing for," he went on. "Young, plump, and tender. You will be my main course at dinner tonight." And he seized Pearl in a tight embrace.

"Unhand her, you villain," the bone screamed, "or I'll bite your ears off!"

"Who is that speaking?" asked the surprised fox.

"A ravenous crocodile who dotes on fresh fox chops, that's who!" answered the bone.

The wily fox was not as easily duped as the robbers. He saw no dangerous crocodile. He peered into Pearl's purse, where the sounds seemed to be coming from, and pulled out the bone. "As I live and flourish!" he exclaimed. "A talking bone. I've always wanted to own something of this sort." And he put the bone in his pocket, where it roared and ranted to no avail.

Pushing Pearl along, the fox set out for his hideaway. Pearl's sobs were so pitiful the fox couldn't help feeling a little sorry for her, but he was determined she would be his dinner.

"Please, Mr. Fox," Pearl whimpered, "may I have my bone back, at least until I have to die?"

"Oh, all right," said the fox, disgusted with himself for being so soft-hearted, and he handed her the bone, which she put back in her purse.

"You must let this beautiful young creature go on living," the bone yelled. "Have you no shame, sir!"

The fox laughed. "Why should I be ashamed? I can't help being the way I am. I didn't make the world."

The bone commenced to revile the fox. "You coward!" it sneered. "You worm, you odoriferous wretch!"

These expletives were annoying. "Shut up, or I'll eat you," the fox snarled. "It would be amusing to gnaw on a bone that talks . . . and screams with pain."

The bone kept quiet the rest of the way, and so did Pearl.

When they arrived at the fox's hideaway, he shoved Pearl, with her bone, into an empty room and locked the door. Pearl sat on the floor and stared at the walls.

"I know how you feel," the bone whispered.

"I'm only just beginning to live," Pearl whispered back. "I don't want it to end."

"I know," said the bone.

"Isn't there something we can do?" Pearl asked.

"I wish I could think of something," said the bone, "but I can't. I feel miserable."

"What's *that*?" Pearl asked. She'd heard some sounds from the kitchen.

"He's sharpening a knife," the bone whispered.

"Oh, my goodness!" Pearl sobbed. "And what's *that*?"

"Sounds like wood being put into a stove," answered the bone.

"I hope it won't all take too long," said Pearl. She could smell vinegar and oil. The fox was preparing a salad to go with his meal. Pearl hugged the bone to her breast. "Bone, say something to comfort me."

"You are very dear to me," said the bone.

"Oh, how dear you are to me!" Pearl replied. She could hear a key in the lock and was unable to get another word out of her throat or turn her eyes toward the door.

"Be brave," the bone whispered. Pearl could only tremble.

She was dragged into the kitchen, where she could see flames in the open stove.

"I regret having to do this to you," sighed the fox. "It's nothing personal."

"*Yibbam!*" said the bone suddenly, without knowing why he said it.

"What was that?" said the fox, standing stock-still.

"Yibbam sibibble!" the bone intoned. "Jibrakken sibibble digray!" And something quite unexpected took place. The fox grew several inches shorter.

"Alabam chinook beboppit gebozzle!" the bone continued, and miraculously the fox was the size of a rabbit. No one could believe what was happening, not Pearl, not the fox, not even the bone, whose words were making it happen.

"Adoonis ishgoolak keebokkin yibapp!" it went on. The fox, clothes and all, was now the size of a mouse.

"Scrabboonit!" the bone ordered, and the mouse—that is, the minuscule fox—scurried away and into a hole.

"I didn't know you could do magic!" Pearl breathlessly exclaimed.

"Neither did I," said the bone.

"Well, what made you say those words?"

"I wish I knew," the bone said. "They just came to me, I *had* to say them. I must have picked them up somehow, hanging around with that witch."

"You're an amazing bone," said Pearl, "and this is a day I won't ever forget!"

It was dark when they reached Pearl's house. The moment the door swung open she was in her mother's arms, and right after that in her father's.

"Where on earth have you been?" they both wanted to know. "We were frazzled with worry."

Pearl didn't know what to say first. She held up the bone. "This bone," she said, "can talk!" And just as she had expected, her mother said, "A talking bone? Why, Pearl, it's only your imagination." And her father said something similar. And also as Pearl had expected, the bone astonished them both by remarking, "You have an exceptional daughter."

Before her parents had a chance to get over their shock, Pearl began telling the story of her day's adventure, and the bone helped out. It was all too much for Pearl's parents. Until they got used to it.

The bone stayed on and became part of the family. It was given an honored place in a silver tray on the mantelpiece. Pearl always took it to bed when she retired, and the two chatterboxes whispered together until late in the night. Sometimes the bone put Pearl to sleep by singing, or by imitating soft harp music.

Anyone who happened to be alone in the house always had the bone to converse with. And they all had music whenever they wanted it, and sometimes even when they didn't.